YAFIC
25.99
OCT 03 201

To the friends who have helped me through dark times.

Boy Seeking Band is published by Stone Arch Books
1710 Roe Crest Drive, North Mankato, Minnesota 56003
www.mycapstone.com

Cataloging-in-Publication Data is available on the Library of Congress website.
ISBN: 978-1-4965-4447-6 (library hardcover)
ISBN: 978-1-4965-4451-3 (eBook)

Summary: In the middle of eighth grade, prodigy bass player Terence Kato is
forced to transfer from a private arts school to a public school, where the kids
seemingly speak a different language. Luckily, Terence knows a universal one:
music. He quickly sets out to build a rock band and, in the process, make a few
friends. First up: a SINGER.

Cover illustration and design by Brann Garvey

Printed in the United States of America.
010368F17

SINGER WANTED

BY STEVE BREZENOFF

STONE ARCH BOOKS
a capstone imprint

TABLE OF CONTENTS

INTRODUCTION

Terence Kato is a prodigy bass player, but he's determined to finish middle school on a high note. Life has other plans. In the middle of eighth grade, he's forced to transfer from a private arts school to a public school, where the kids seemingly speak a different language. Luckily, Terence knows a universal one: music. He quickly sets out to build the city's greatest rock band.

First up: a SINGER.

CHAPTER ONE

On the corner of Whatever Street and I Wish I Didn't Live Here Lane stands Terence Kato. He leans against a stop sign and watches as a school bus rolls by, brakes two blocks up, and lets on five kids the boy doesn't know. To be honest, Terence has no interest in ever knowing them.

By all rights, he ought to be on that bus, though. He should be seated next to some snot-covered, public-school kid who probably wouldn't know the circle of fifths if it rolled him over. But he's not.

Of course, it's also true that Terence's dad should be awake in time to drive his son to his first day at Franklin Middle School. But that's not happening either.

So instead, Terence pushes off the stop sign, hitches his bass guitar onto his shoulder, and heads around the back of his new house to fetch his bike.

"Later, Dad," Terence says to the drab, little rent-a-home as he rolls away. With every bump, stop, and practically every pedal, the bass guitar bounces hard against his back like some sort of punishment. But he has to bring it. First of all, he preregistered for the after-school band program and couldn't show up to the first day without an instrument. Second, wearing a gig bag attracts attention — the kind of attention he'll need if he has any hope of starting a band at Franklin, like the band he had back at Hart Arts, and entering the battle of the youth bands in the spring.

As Terence pulls up to the bike rack, which is full, he hears a bell ring. He quickly chains his bike to a No Parking sign and runs inside.

The halls are quiet. Empty. He's late.

Inside the school's front office, a man behind the counter stares at a computer screen and speaks quietly into a headset. "Excuse me?" Terence says. The man doesn't look up.

Terence adjusts the strap on his gig bag and notices a surly-looking girl slouching in the metal chair behind him. She has dark skin, short hair, and a suspicious golden piercing in her nose. He's pretty sure she's staring at him, probably plotting when to knock him over the head and take his phone and wallet.

That's what they do in public schools: they beat you up and steal your stuff.

"Um, excuse me?" Terence repeats, trying to get the man's attention by waving his schedule around noisily. "It's my first day, and I'm late. I don't know where I'm supposed to be."

"He won't help you," says a voice behind him. Terence doesn't turn around, but he knows it's the scowling girl. "All day, every day, he's on that phone, doing who knows what, ignoring every student that walks in here."

Terence still doesn't turn around. "Did I ask you?" he mutters under his breath.

"No," the girl says. "But I'm a very generous person, so I'm helping you anyway."

"How are you helping me right now?" Terence asks, and he finally turns around to find the girl standing right behind him.

She's taller than him, which is nothing new. The Katos are a short family, but Terence's dad assures him that he'll have a growth spurt any day now and catch up — at least to the girls. Although Terence doubts he'll ever catch up to this particular girl.

"Let me see that," she says, snatching his schedule.

"Hey!" Terence says, but the girl turns

around and blocks him from getting the paper back while she reads it.

"Terence Kato," she reads aloud, and then says over her shoulder, "Aren't you a little short to be an eighth grader?"

"Give it back."

"OK, OK," the girl says, finally handing him the paper. "Anyway, you missed advisory, but your first hour is in the same room. I can show you — if you want help."

Terence glares at her a moment and then glances at the man behind the desk, who still hasn't looked up.

"Fine," Terence mutters, and then even more quietly, "Thanks."

"No problem, Terry," she says. "I'm Meredith Carson, by the way. But you can call me —"

"Merry?" Terence interrupts as he follows her out of the office.

"Eddie, actually," she says. "Anyone calls me Merry, I knife 'em."

Terence flinches.

Eddie laughs.

"I'm kidding, newbie," she says and then adds, "Or am I?

Terence isn't sure, really.

Eddie laughs again. "I take it from that Cadillac strapped to your back you'll be joining our esteemed band?"

"It's my bass guitar!" Terence explains, his voice going higher and louder with excitement. "Are you in the band? What do you play?"

"Easy, eager beaver," Eddie says. "You know band class isn't until *after* school, right? It's extracurricular."

"I know," Terence says. "But my bass didn't fit in my locker, and I didn't know where else to put it."

She sizes him up. "Bet you would, though," she says. "Fit in your locker, I mean."

Terence feels his face go hot as she leads him around a corner. They head up to the school's second floor, and she stops in front of the first door: 212.

"This is your room, band boy," she says. "Have fun." With that, she leaves him standing in front of the closed door to his first public-school class since fifth grade.

He sneaks a look in the window. The tables are set up in clusters of four. Walking among the tables with her hands behind her back is —

Terence takes a quick look at his schedule: Ms. Hardison, his new math teacher.

"OK, you can do this," he whispers to himself as he leans on the wall next to the door. "Of course, if everyone in there is as nice and 'helpful' as *Meredith* was, this might be the worst hour of my life."

Suddenly, the door flies open and Ms. Hardison pokes out her head. "Will you be joining us this morning, Mr. Kato," she says, "or do you have a soliloquy to rehearse out here?"

"Oh, um . . . ," Terence mumbles, not because he doesn't know what a soliloquy is; Hart Arts had a renowned drama department. In fact, Polly Winger, the singer from his band at Hart, had been one of the department's top stars, even though she was only in eighth grade.

Terence missed his old school and his old life. But most of all, he missed the Kato Quintet. They were his best friends and the best band at Hart Arts. Sure, they were only miles away, but they might as well have been on another planet.

"Sorry," Terence finally says. "I had trouble finding the room."

Ms. Hardison steps to one side and holds the door open for him, smirking. "Welcome to Franklin Middle," she says as he passes, dodging the top of his gig bag. "What *is* that?"

The class laughs as Terence finds an empty desk in one of the clusters. "It's my bass guitar," he says. "It didn't fit in my locker."

"Just lean it in the corner," Ms. Hardison says, not bothering to hide her contempt for Terence's extra baggage.

Terence obeys and then slumps into his seat. His cluster-mates don't even look at him.

CHAPTER TWO

Terence's first day at Franklin Middle is
as long and arduous as the first five minutes.
Without Eddie as a tour guide, he's late to every
class — even lunch. The one brief moment of
pleasantness during his day is Music.

The teacher, Mr. Bonn, plays piano for
forty-five minutes straight, practically, and
the students sing with varying degrees of
enthusiasm. To be honest, Terence is probably
somewhere in the middle, and even the most

enthusiastic singers in the room aren't nearly as good as Polly.

Almost no one is, Terence thinks as Mr. Bonn takes a brief pause between the end of the Beatles' "Here Comes the Sun" and the start of A Great Big World's "Hold Each Other."

Terence and Polly did "Hold Each Other" in rehearsals once, long ago — six weeks ago, in fact. Terence did the rap. It was hilarious.

But Music class is less than an hour of Terence's first six-and-a-half-hour day, and Music alone cannot save it.

At 3:45, Terence hurries along Franklin Middle's back hallway. It slopes downward into the cooler underbelly: the basement, home to the school's utility room, storage, and "important" departments like Fine Arts and Music. He can hear a handful of other players warming up, and though they don't sound like half the talent he knew back at Hart Arts, it's still music to his ears.

Terence's heart races as he picks up his pace. He's almost jogging by the time he finds the orchestra room and hurries through the double doors.

Everyone stops and looks up at him: the stranger with the gig bag on his back.

"Um, hi," Terence says, carefully pulling the bass from his shoulder and holding it in front of him like a shield. "This is band, right?"

The dozen or so students gape at him, their saxophones, trumpets, and drumsticks stuck in limbo between being played and being set down.

"I'm —" he starts to add.

"Terence Kato!" says a booming voice.

"Yes?" Terence says, and then spots a giant man striding toward him from the back of the room. The man is easily six and a half feet tall and nearly as wide. He wears a walrus-like mustache, a brown corduroy suit that he's managed to sweat through, and a pair of thick, oversized eyeglasses.

The man wipes his hands on a cream-colored chamois as he thunders across the room like a walking tree. "We've been expecting you."

Terence glances again at the agape band members. "You have?"

"I'm Kenny Bonk," the giant man booms, "and of course!" He drops the chamois and walks back to the black metal music stand that serves as his conductor's podium. "Join the group. I see you brought your bass."

Terence nods.

"Didn't fit in your locker, did it?" calls a boy from the risers.

Terence looks up and spots him, a big baritone sax leaning on his hip.

"Mine either," the boy says, patting the sax's curved, shining top.

"That's Jordan," Mr. Bonk says. "You'll meet all the players, but for now we can get started. You're running a little late?"

"A little," Terence admits. He spots a bass

amp beside the risers and makes a beeline for the chair closest to it, unzipping his gig bag as he goes.

"You can store your instrument here," Mr. Bonk says, "if you don't want to carry it back and forth each night. But you strike me as the kind of player who likes to practice every night. Am I right?"

"Um, yeah, I guess," Terence admits, but his face goes hot as he goes on, "but I have another bass at home I'll use to practice."

"Ah!" Mr. Bonk loosens his knit tie. "Life in private school, eh?"

Terence feels the eyes of his bandmates on him as he plugs in and fiddles with the amp's knobs.

Mr. Bonk pulls off his sweat-drenched jacket and tosses it aside. His undershirt is soaked through as well.

"Let's start with 'Don't Mean a Thing,'" he prompts the class.

Terence actually smiles as he checks his tuning. The song is a Duke Ellington classic, perhaps the standardest standard of all jazz standards. Terence could play the bass part in his sleep. He probably has.

The rest of the band members, though, shuffle through sheet music, fuss with their stands, and look up at Mr. Bonk. The song often starts with just a piano intro, but this jazz band has no piano, and the sheet music probably comes from an arranger who specializes in school-band music, which means keeping things simple and plain.

"And a one, and a two," Mr. Bonk announces, raising his baton. When he enthusiastically lowers it with a strong jerk of his head, the band leaps into the song with all the swing and vivacity of a bowl of cold spaghetti without sauce. Even without melted butter.

Terence keeps his head down and runs through the bass line, but it's difficult playing a version of "It Don't Mean a Thing" with surprisingly little swing.

When the song is over, Mr. Bonk pauses for a moment, then looks at Terence and smiles somewhat politely.

Here it comes, Terence thinks. *He'll tell me how great I am, and how lucky I was to go to Hart for a few years, and I'll be all embarrassed. Just try to smile.*

"Mr. Kato," Mr. Bonk booms. "The others and I have been practicing 'Don't Mean a Thing' for a few weeks now from the sheet music provided. It would really help us if you could stick to the bass line as written."

"Thanks, I —" Terence starts, but then catches himself. "Wait — what?"

"There's a copy under your chair," Mr. Bonk points out, "along with the rest of our repertoire."

Terence reaches down and finds a short stack of sheet music.

"It Don't Mean a Thing" is right on top. Under that, "A Night in Tunisia," "Here's that Rainy Day," and "Manteca."

They're all classics. Terence would in fact love to be in a jazz band that played those numbers. Unfortunately, it happens to be *this* particular jazz band.

For the next forty-five minutes, the Franklin Middle School jazz band plods through their set list, a couple of times each song, and Terence nobly plucks along with them on his song-sheet-appointed bass line.

The exercise is utterly exhausting, and when it's over, Terence unplugs and packs, leaving his bagged bass in the back room per Mr. Bonk's instructions. Then he hurries from the music room amid stares from the rest of the band.

The basement halls are empty, and the school seems darker now. His footsteps echo as he struggles to recall the way back up to the main floor and the school's front doors.

"I think it's this way," Terence mutters, jiggling his keys, anxious to get back to his bike, unlock it, and ride home.

No, not home. *Just* house, Terence thinks. *That place will never be my real home.*

Terence turns right. *It must be this way.* Then he turns left and finds a stairwell, but the double doors are locked.

He goes straight, then turns left, and then left again — another dead end at a locked, black, unmarked door.

"Great," he says, thumping the locked door with his fist. Then he adds, "Thanks a lot, Mom," though he knows none of this is any of her fault.

Terence slides down the wall and lets his book bag fall to the floor beside him. "Sorry," he whispers, an apology to his mom. He misses her still; he will forever, he sees now.

Right after she died, Terence imagined that the missing — the pain he felt immediately after her death — would eventually stop, like getting over a very bad cold or something.

Turns out, mourning doesn't work that way. After six months, the pain is still like a tickle in his throat, ready to become a full-on flu at any moment.

Terence sniffs back tears and readies himself to find a way out of this middle school maze. But as he does, a faraway voice rises in the silence of the basement.

A girl's voice — singing.

For a moment, Terence sits frozen, too stunned to move. A single tear stalls in the corner of his right eye as if it too is caught up in the reverberating voice: *"Maybe . . . I should have saved those leftover dreams."*

A split second later, Terence leaps to his feet, wipes the swollen tear from his eye, and grabs his bag. It knocks against his leg as he runs up the hall, desperately seeking the singer.

Instead, Terence finds abandoned hallways,

echoing with vibrato and spinning him in maddening circles.

Before long, he's back at the orchestra room, but now the double doors are locked, the lights are off, and no one's around. Terence pauses a moment, his back against the locked doors, and tries to get a fix on the voice, but it quickly fades, and before long he can't tell if he hears it all, or if it's just an echo in his mind: *"Funny, that rainy day is here."*

And a moment later, silence.

This time, when Terence steps away from the orchestra room, he winds through the basement hallways and finds the ramp right away. In moments, he's on the first floor and at the front door, amid the cacophony of extracurricular students, basketball players and cross-country runners, after-school advisors, and office-hour department heads.

Terence pushes past all of them and through the front doors into a cloudburst, and though in moments he drenched, he doesn't care. His bass is safely inside, after all.

Besides, at the moment, he's more concerned that the No Parking sign, twenty paces down the sidewalk from Franklin Middle School, no longer has a bike chained to it.

Still, he drudges through the rain and grabs hold of the signpost, as if testing its very existence.

"Hey, Terry!" comes a girl's voice from behind him, one not nearly as spellbinding as the vocalist in the basement.

Terence turns around, knowing full well who he'll find standing just inside the open door. "Merry Eddie," he grumbles.

"You miss the late bus, new kid?" she calls through the rain at him as he plods through puddles back to the door.

"My bike was stolen," he says, though that has nothing to do with the late bus, which he didn't know anything about until this moment.

Besides, he's not about to admit he got lost in the basement. He drops his bag as he steps through the door she holds open for him.

"Nah, not stolen," she says. "Impounded. You're not allowed to chain up to signs."

Terence slides down the locker closest to the door and pulls out his phone. "Now you tell me," he says as he selects Dad from his contacts.

"Aw," Eddie says, sliding down next to him. "You'll get it back. Don't worry. They'll make you fill out a form in the morning."

"Who?" Terence says.

Eddie nods toward the main office. "Them."

"Great," Terence says, recalling his experience in the office that morning.

After the fifth ring, Dad picks up. "Hello?" he says in a familiar, groggy voice.

"Dad?" Terence says. "Were you sleeping?"

At the same moment, a tall boy Terence recognizes from jazz band steps up to him and Eddie and says, "All right, I'm ready. Let's go."

"No," Dad says, forcing cheery wakefulness into his voice. "No, of course not. Where are you?" And a moment later, "Did I miss pickup? I'm sorry —"

"No, Dad," Terence says. "I'll explain later, but can you pick me up?"

"See ya, Terry," Eddie says, getting to her feet.

"Wait a second," Terence starts.

But Dad interrupts him, and Eddie and the boy disappear through the front doors. "I'll be there right away. I just have to —"

"Get up and get dressed?" Terence finishes.

Dad sighs. "Gimme a break, kid," he says. "I'm doing my best."

Terence takes a deep breath and stands up. "I know," he says, looking through the glass doors.

For a moment, the rain has stopped.

CHAPTER THREE

Dinner that night is what Dad calls FFY: "Fend For Yourself." It used to be something special, back when Dad *and* Mom called it that. Basically, Terence could make anything he wanted — mini pizzas, mac and cheese out of the box, or PB&Js — and Dad would get the night off from cooking.

But Dad has had the night off from making supper for months now, and FFY isn't cute anymore. Terence takes his mini pizzas — English muffins topped with American cheese and ketchup — to his tiny bedroom and dumps his homework onto the bed.

None of it is music homework, but Terence pulls his bass out from under the bed, and plugs in anyway. He turns the volume down, fiddles with the EQ, and runs through every scale he can think of until he nearly falls asleep.

The next morning, Terence shovels down his bowl of cereal, doesn't bother to wake Dad, and takes his chances on the bus. His stop is one of the first, so he manages to snag a seat to himself in the middle: the invisible section of the bus.

In the middle, you're not some butt-kissing weirdo who wants to sit right up close and personal with the bus driver, but you're also not interested in the hijinks, spitballs, and phone videos being shared in the back.

Two stops later, though, to Terence's surprise, someone shoves in his bag and sits down next to him. Terence doesn't look up. He just pushes against the window, stares outside, turns up Joni Mitchell's *Hejira* on his noise-canceling headphones, and hopes it's clear that he's not interested in making friends.

For a minute, his plan works. After all, most people climbing onto this Franklin Middle bus aren't out to develop new relationships first thing in the morning. But soon his new seat neighbor grabs his arm and gives him a shake.

Terence looks down to find long fingers wrapped around his forearm, adorned with cheap, quarter-machine rings. The nails are painted every color of the rainbow and chipped. He's not surprised when he lifts his eyes and find's Eddie's expectant face, her lips moving in mock frustration desperately saying *something* over and over.

Terence rolls his eyes and pulls off his headphones in the middle of the title track — his favorite. Eddie's mouth keeps moving, silently, and slowly bends into a smile.

"You're hilarious."

"Sorry," Eddie says. "Couldn't resist." She nods toward the headphones. "Can I listen?"

Terence shrugs and hands over the headphones. Eddie puts them on, listens for a moment, and then says in a way-too-loud, headphone-wearing voice, "What is this?"

Half the bus turns around to look at them. Terence grabs back his headphones. "It's Joni Mitchell," he says, shrinking lower in the seat. "Keep your voice down."

"Sorry, sorry," she says. "It's weird. Are you weird?"

"Sure," he says, hanging the headphones around his neck as he switches off the music. "I'm super weird. You should probably sit somewhere else."

Eddie laughs, and the bus jerks and screeches to a stop at the curb in front of the school. "See you, weird Terry," Eddie says as she practically leaps out of the seat.

Terence watches as she catches up with a
boy — the same boy she left school with
yesterday. The boy glares at Terence and,
Terence swears, growls.

Terence thinks about ditching jazz band that
afternoon. He wonders whether remaining
a member of such an unfocused, untalented
group would be detrimental to his playing in the
long run. Two thoughts stop him from skipping:
One, what if he never gets a band together?
He'd have no one to play with except himself.
And two, if he goes to band practice there's a
chance that he'll find the girl with the echoing
voice, the voice he needs for his band.

Terence arrives on time this afternoon, and
while he unpacks his bass, he glances up at the
sax player — it's the kid who picked up Eddie
yesterday and escorted her off the bus this
morning. He doesn't know this guy, but it's a

safe guess that he's Eddie's brother. If Terence knows just one other student at this school — and he does know *exactly* one other student — it's Eddie.

Surely her brother will talk to him?

"Hey," Terence says as the bigger boy slips on his saxophone's mouthpiece and tests the reed quietly.

The boy looks up, his eyebrows furrowed and his lips tight around the reed of his sax.

"Hey," Terence tries again. "You know any singers?"

The boy pulls the mouthpiece out a fraction of inch, opens his mouth as if he might speak, but then instead draws in a huge breath and starts playing the opening bass line of Pink Floyd's "Money."

Terence stands there a minute, anticipating a genuine response, but when the boy closes his eyes — like he's really feeling the music — Terence gives up and goes back to his bass.

The jazz bands runs through their repertoire again, each number twice, until it's 4:30 and the late buses are due to leave. Terence is the quickest to pack up.

He sprints from the room into the cavernous basement hallways — and smack into Eddie. He knocks a cup of coffee from her hand, sending the chocolaty-brown liquid splashing to the ground.

"Whoa, Weird Terry!" she snaps. "Watch it."

"Sorry!" Terence says. "I was hurrying and —"

Eddie crouches and drops a handful of paper napkins on the spill. "It's fine," she says, though from the tone of her voice, he can tell it's anything but.

"Did I get your boots?" he asks. It's hard to tell because they're a little worn — in a cool way, of course. "Your pants?"

"It's fine," she repeats. "You can owe me for the coffee. And go get some paper towels."

Terence scans the hallway and spots the nearest boys' room. "On it," he says, dropping his book bag against the wall and taking off down the hall.

The restroom is a mess. The paper towel dispenser is not only empty but knocked clear off the wall. Thinking quickly, Terence bangs open the stall, pulls loose a big handful of toilet paper, and hurries back to the scene of the collision.

Eddie is gone.

Terence's bag leans against the wall a few feet from a pile of mocha-soaked napkins. He drops to his knees beside the remaining mess and wipes at it with the toilet paper, which quickly disintegrates in his hands. Terence sighs, gathers the mushy mess, and tosses the whole wad away in the boys' room trash can.

When he gets back to his bag and throws it onto his shoulder, the voice from the day before returns: it's clearer today, closer — even nearby.

This time the song is "It Don't Mean a Thing (If It Ain't Got That Swing)."

Terence brightens at once. He sprints up the nearby ramp and rounds the corner. The voice is so close.

At the top of the ramp, two backlit figures walk away from him toward the sunlight of the main floor: he is tall and lurching, like a half-ape; she is not quite as tall, and lean-looking and strong. And she's singing.

"Wait!" Terence calls up the ramp as he runs. "Wait up, you two!"

They stop and turn, and Terence still can't see their faces because the setting sun is like an orange and pink spotlight behind them, shining right into his eyes.

"Was that you?" he says, squinting and shielding his eyes, as he looks at the girl. "Were you just singing?" He looks over his shoulder into the basement. "Back there?"

The girl seems to glance at the boy beside

her as Terence moves up the ramp toward them. Something clicks then, only an instant, before the angle of the sun changes so he can clearly see who's standing at the top of the ramp.

"Eddie?" Terence says, and beside her, the growling saxophone player from jazz band.

"You following me, Weird Terry?" Eddie asks. She doesn't look amused — or flattered.

"Who is this guy?" asks the big guy. Terence decides it must be her brother.

"Oh, some new kid," Eddie says, glaring at Terence. "He's harmless."

Terence swallows his pride and asks again: "Was that you singing in the basement a minute ago? 'Don't Mean a Thing'?"

She shrugs one shoulder. "Yeah, so?"

"Can I talk to you a second?" Terence asks, and off her brother's ice-cold stare adds, "In private?"

Eddie sighs, and then says to her brother, "Don't let the bus leave without me."

He growls but turns and walks toward the front doors, where the late bus is probably already idling. The bus is Terence's ride home too, since his bike is still in the hands of Franklin Middle School's powers-that-be.

"So what's up?" Eddie says, striding down the ramp to meet him. "And make it quick."

She stares at him with the patience of a hungry lioness being kept from her meal — and Terence feels like that meal.

Terence takes a deep breath. "Look," he finally says, closing his eyes and clenching his teeth, "I'm new here. You don't like me. I get it. I'm not out to make friends."

"Wow," Eddie says, and Terence goes on.

"I'm hopefully only here a few months, after all. But there is one thing I need to survive even that long, and that's a band."

"A band?"

Terence nods. "I play bass," he says, "and a few other things. I'm open as far as genre and lineup, but there's one thing I'll need, and that's a great singer. You're a great singer."

"I know," Eddie says, still unsmiling.

"Um," Terence says, because he kind of thought that would fluster her at least a *little* bit. "So what I'm asking is . . ."

"I know what you're asking," Eddie says as she backs away, up the ramp. Her brother has appeared at the top again to glower at them. "You want me to join your band, which doesn't exist yet."

"Yeah," Terence says, though she's managed to make it sound silly.

Eddie reaches the top of the ramp and turns her back on him. "I'll think about it," she says.

"I need you!" Terence calls after her as she and her brother walk off. "Um, that didn't come out right."

Her brother snarls over his shoulder at Terence. Eddie calls down the ramp, "You better get on the bus. It won't wait."

With that, she and her brother vanish down the hallway.

"No, thanks!" Terence calls after them, though he's sure they can't hear him. "I'll get a ride . . . somehow." The thought of getting onto the bus with her after that awkwardness makes his stomach turn, so he pulls out his phone and calls Dad to wake him.

He picks up after the fifth ring. "Terence?" he mumbles, the sleep still in his voice.

"Dad," Terence says as he climbs the ramp toward the front door. He watches the bus pull away. "Remind me again why Mom didn't have life insurance."

Dad sighs. "You need a ride?"

"Yeah."

"Ten minutes," Dad says, and the phone clicks off in Terence's hand.

CHAPTER FOUR

First thing the next morning, Terence heads to the main office to try to get his bike back. Eddie's not there, and Terence idly wonders why she was there on his first day. Did she get in trouble a lot?

The man who ignored Terence the other morning is back at his desk — or maybe he never left his desk — talking into his headset.

"Excuse me," Terence says, leaning a little on the counter. "My bike was confiscated a couple of days ago."

The man glances oh-so-briefly at Terence, but he doesn't say anything to him. He doesn't even pull off his headset as if he plans to listen to anything the boy says.

"I didn't know you're not allowed to chain up bikes there," Terence goes on.

The man ignores him.

"Is there a form I need to fill out, or . . . ," Terence says, but the question is drowned out by the sound of the bell to start advisory period.

The man looks up at Terence, points at the bell on the wall, and goes back to his call.

"Thanks," Terence says. "Thanks a lot."

The morning goes well enough, certainly better than his first morning. Terence is beginning to get a feel for the rhythm of this school — so different from Hart Arts.

At Hart, the core classes — like math, language arts, and science — were reserved for rotating classes after lunch.

Terence spent all morning before lunch in one classroom, with music instructors and other students majoring in music performance and theory. The room contained a pair of pianos, a range of percussion instruments, brass, woodwind, strings, and any other instrument you can imagine — there and for the playing.

Many mornings, Dr. Orderall declared an hour as free-play, and it wasn't the free-play he had in kindergarten. It was spontaneous rock trios blasting through hard-rock covers, wild jazz quintets riffing on a Gershwin melody, or even a string quartet swaying to Bach.

At Franklin Middle School, Terence is pretty sure a morning like that might be so off-the-wall that even the man in the office would hang up his phone and come out from behind the desk just to see what is going on.

Still, by lunch on his third day at Franklin, Terence understands how the school works. The classes are, for the most part, entirely boring, but they keep the classes short so students can tolerate the boredom. That makes sense.

Earlier this morning, Terence didn't feel like making lunch for himself — and Dad was still asleep on the couch — so he's stuck with the hot lunch. He lines up.

"So, I've been thinking about it," says a familiar voice behind him.

Terence turns and finds Eddie leaning against the wall. "About what?" Terence says, though he knows she means his band that doesn't exist yet.

"You know you don't have to get the hot lunch," she says, rolling along the wall on one shoulder as the line shimmies up.

"OK," Terence says. "That's not what I thought you'd been thinking about."

"It's not," Eddie says. "But, I mean — least I can do. You should skip this — what is it today? Pot roast? — and hit the snack bar instead."

"What's the snack bar?" Terence asks.

Eddie rolls her eyes. She has very big eyes. "Come on," she says, taking his hand and pulling him out of the line.

She leads him in between tables and around the corner.

"I . . . ," Terence begins, gaping at the crowded corner of hidden tables, "had no idea this was here."

"That's my fault, actually," Eddie says. She takes him past the tables to a doorway on the far side. A sign hanging above it reads "Snack Bar."

"Whoa," Terence says, because there's a bagel line, a pizza line, a fryer line, and racks of chips, fresh fruit, and premade sandwiches and salads.

"Right?" Eddie says. "No reason to eat from the hot line . . . unless you have one of those lunch cards. They don't take them here."

Terence's skin goes cold. *He* has one of those prepaid lunch cards. Somehow his dad actually remembered to sign him up for one before he started at Franklin, and it's got all his lunch money on it.

Eddie catches on quick, and her mouth falls open. She covers it with one hand. "Oh! I'm sorry."

Terence shakes his head and smiles. "It's fine," he says, struggling to remember if there's any actual money in his wallet today. "I do have a card, but I have some cash too. I mean, I can buy something. Probably."

Eddie sighs, like it's a huge relief, and scampers up to the bagel counter. "Plain with cream cheese and an extra cream cheese."

"That's fifty—" the man behind the counter starts.

Eddie cuts him off. "Fifty cents extra, I know, I know," she says, and then glances at Terence over her shoulder. "What are you having?"

"Same as you, I guess?" he says.

Eddie orders another and pulls folded bills from the front pocket of her jeans. "It's on me."

"No, really," Terence begins to object, hurrying to the cash register.

Eddie blocks him with her body. "Really, it's the least I could do, Weird Terry."

"What, because you won't join my band?"

"Join?" Eddie says, laying her bills on the stainless counter. The cashier scoops them up and sucks her teeth as she counts. "You mean *found*. That's the word when you start a band with someone."

"Fine, *found* then."

"First of all, who said I'm not going to found a band with you?" Eddie says, putting out her hand for the change. "Second of all, that's not why it's the least I can do."

"Then why?" Terence says.

Eddie pockets her change and hands Terence a paper tray with a bagel and two little covered cups of cream cheese. He can see at once why she asked for an extra. They're tiny.

"Did you ever wonder," Eddie says as she

leaves the snack bar, Terence hurrying along behind her, "why I was in the office the other morning?"

"Actually, yes," Terence says. "I figured you were in trouble for something?"

She drops an icy glare before taking a seat at the end of a crowded table. Terence sits across from her, next to a boy he recognizes from his math class. Or maybe science.

"I wasn't in trouble," Eddie says. "I don't *get* in trouble."

"You don't?" Terence says, squeaking in surprise.

"Is that so shocking?"

"Well, with the way you dress and . . . ," Terence stops, and then adds, "and your hair."

"Oh, please," Eddie says. "I'm unique, not criminal. In fact, I'm such a good student and so popular with the teachers and the principal that they chose *me* to meet the new student and show him around."

"What?" Terence says, loud enough so the other kids at the table look over at him.

Eddie laughs.

"What?" Terence repeats, whispering this time. "You were *supposed* to be helping me?"

She shrugs. "Yeah, and in fact way more than I did. I was supposed to hook up with you at lunch, help you find your way, even make sure you got to the bus — or the *late* bus — on time. Maybe I should have warned you about locking up your bike in the wrong place too."

Terence leans back in his chair. "I can't believe this."

"I know," Eddie says, nodding. "But look. We didn't exactly hit it off. I figured we'd both be better off if I just left you alone."

Terence thinks back to his confiscated bike, the rainstorm, and the late bus he didn't even know existed this time two days ago. "You were wrong."

"I know," Eddie says again. "I'm sorry."

Terence picks up his bagel. "I need a knife."

"Are you threatening me?"

"No, to spread the cream cheese," Terence says.

Eddie shakes her head. "Like this." She tears off a chunk of her bagel, rips open the top of one of her cream cheese cups, and dips the chunk of bagel. "See?"

Terence copies her and pops a big chunk of bagel into his mouth. "At least there's one thing here better than at Hart," he says as he chews. "Lunch was awful. My mom made me bag lunch every day."

"Just the food?" Eddie says. "What about me?"

Terence shrugs, but he thinks about Polly Winger back at Hart, and about Simon and Jalen — the old band. *His* old band. "I guess you should probably audition," he finally says.

Eddie gives him a shocked look. "Didn't you hear me sing already?"

"Yeah, but I mean," Terence says, "the acoustics in the basement are pretty crazy. The reverb can be very . . . forgiving."

"Oh, please," Eddie says, tearing a piece of her bagel like she's tearing his head off. "Anyway, you have a lot of other people lining up to *found* this band with you?"

"Sure," Terence says. "You're not the only person I've met here, you know."

"Ha!" Eddie says. "Name one other."

Terence scrambles through his mind, struggling to recall the name of even one classmate, but he's too slow.

"See?" Eddie says.

"Still," Terence says. "You should audition. Can you meet me in the orchestra room before jazz band later?"

Eddie looks down at her bagel and seems to shrink into her chair. "Fine," she says quietly. "But if anyone else shows up, I'm not doing it."

Terence almost laughs.

"You're scared to sing in front of people?"

"So?" Eddie says, looking up at him.

"Nothing," he says. "Lots of people get stage fright. It's just funny because you sing in the hall every day."

"I didn't know anyone was listening," Eddie says shyly.

Terence sits for a beat, looking at the girl across from him. She's easily six inches taller than him, dressed like she couldn't care less what anyone thinks, and has an amazing singing voice. But performing scares her. Might make the battle of the bands a little trickier.

"Anyway," he finally says. "We should have a few minutes. Enough for one song."

And just like that, her shy moment passes. She sits up straight, excited. "What songs do you know?"

"Lots of songs," Terence says. "I have a whole set list from my band back home — I mean, back at Hart."

"I know everything the jazz band has done for the last three years," she says. "My twin brother, Luke, joined in sixth grade, and I steal his sheet music."

"The big guy who plays sax?" Terence says.

Eddie nods as she pops the last of her bagel into her mouth.

"You got all the talent in the family?" Terence asks before he can stop himself, and feels his face go red.

Eddie smiles at him as she pushes her chair back. "He's not very good, is he?" she admits. "Anyway, see if you can sneak out of last hour a little early," she adds. "To make sure we have time."

"Sure," Terence says, watching her leave, though he has no idea how to sneak out early.

It's 3:25 that afternoon, and Ms. Holyoake is lecturing about different economic systems and the formation of the European Union. School ends in fifteen minutes, and five minutes after that the jazz band will turn up for practice.

It's now or never. Terence puts up his hand.

"Yes . . . ?" Ms. H struggles to remember his name.

Terence decides this isn't the best time to remind her. "Can I go to the bathroom?"

Ms. H glances at the clock over the whiteboard. "Can't it wait fifteen minutes?"

Terence opens his mouth to answer but instead just shakes his head. A few snickers crackle in the back of the room, but Terence ignores them.

"Fine, fine, go," Ms. H says, and immediately goes back to her lecture, her colored marker streaking across the whiteboard as she stands with her back to the class.

It's the perfect opportunity. Terence grabs his backpack as secretly as he can and quietly hurries from the room. All he can do is hope none of his classmates will tell Ms. H he took his stuff with him, which means he's obviously not coming back.

The halls are quiet and empty, but Terence knows monitors and security are roaming too — someplace. This is public school, after all. He moves through the corridors like a spy or a ninja, stopping at every corner and peeking carefully around, until he reaches the ramp to the basement and hurries down.

Terence hears her before he sees her. Though he notices she's singing a bit more quietly this afternoon, her voice is unmistakable as she coos the chilling refrain of "Now At Last," made famous by Blossom Dearie. He can tell it's not her typical range or style, but she still sounds good.

Terence stops around the corner from the band room, listening and waiting for her to finish. When she's done, he waits a bit more, and then jogs into view.

"Made it," he says, feigning breathlessness. "How much time do we have?"

"Plenty," Eddie says, crossing her arms, "and I know you were listening around the corner."

"How do you know?" Terence says.

"The light was behind you, genius," she says. "And you have a shadow."

Terence looks down, as if to catch the offending shade in the act. "Oh."

"Yeah, oh," she says, grabbing the band room door handle. "Come on."

They're alone. Mr. Bonk's office is dark, the door closed. Terence goes to the piano and plays the opening riff to "Now At Last."

Eddie rolls her eyes. "You just *heard* that."

"I wanna hear it again," Terence says, smiling. He nods at her as he reaches the vocals entrance, and through a little laughter, Eddie sings.

Polly Winger was a Blossom Dearie fan. Still is, Terence imagines. But when she sang

"Now At Last," she never quite found the song's bittersweet romance. That's why Terence never put the song on the playlist. They stuck with the "fun" Blossom numbers, like "True to You In My Fashion" and "Rhode Island Is Famous for You."

But Eddie nails it. Her voice is light and airy, and even in the ironically poor acoustics of the band room, it sounds full and bright. Terence forces himself to watch the keys as he plays, because though he knows the part well, he doesn't want Eddie to catch him staring at her.

It's a short song, and they slow down together as Eddie sings the last line: *Now at last, I know.*"

Eddie immediately covers her face with her hands.

"That was really good," Terence says quickly.

"Thanks," she says, her voice muffled by her hands. "I know my voice isn't right for Blossom Dearie songs, but —"

"No, it's great," Terence interrupts. "You don't sound like her, but that doesn't matter."

"Really?"

Terence looks back at the piano keys. "Should we do one more?" he says. "We have time."

Eddie bites her lip and nods once.

Terence thinks a minute, and then launches into something completely different. Laughing, Eddie joins in on vocals, and when Mr. Bonk comes in a couple of minutes later, they're knee-deep in a ridiculous cover of Bruno Mars's "Uptown Funk."

Eddie stops singing immediately, but Terence plays on. Mr. Bonk grins and even dances a little as he walks past to unlock his office. "Finish up!" he calls over his shoulder as he disappears inside.

"That was embarrassing," Eddie says, sitting next to Terence on the bench.

Terence slides over a little to make more

room. "Nah, he didn't care," he says. "He probably wishes you'd join the jazz band."

"The jazz band doesn't have a vocalist," Eddie points out.

"Not *yet*," Terence says, but sitting this close to her is making his palms sweat, so he leans back like he's stretching, hops up from the bench, and hurries into Mr. Bonk's office.

"Um, Terence?" she calls after him.

He sticks his head out the door. "Great job. I have to get ready for jazz band now."

"Did I pass the audition?" Eddie says, still sitting at the piano.

"Oh," Terence says. "I'll, um, let you know. Bye!"

And with that, he grabs his bass from the storage area in Bonk's office and waits until he's sure Eddie has left.

CHAPTER FIVE

This is new.

Terence wakes the next morning having dreamed about Eddie: Eddie singing, Eddie laughing, Eddie leading him through the halls of Franklin Middle, Eddie shouting at him angrily and him shouting back.

Of course then he starts crying, and his mom shows up and it's an ordinary dream again, the kind he's been having for the last six months.

"Dad," Terence says, standing at his father's bedside, shaking the man by the shoulders. "Wake up. I need a ride this morning."

Dad rolls over and sits up groggily. He rubs his eyes and gently grabs Terence by the wrist. "What's up? I was up too late again."

"Doing what?" Terence asks, pulling his arm away.

Dad shrugs and stretches and yawns. "Avoiding the bed." He throws his legs over the side of the bed and grabs the bunched-up jeans from the floor. "Give me two minutes, OK?"

Terence nods and heads out to the kitchen. He's eaten already, and he's dressed and ready to go, so he sits at the little table-for-two, puts on his headphones, and brings up the playlist he created last year for Polly. The first song is "It Don't Mean a Thing."

Two minutes in, while Ella Fitzgerald is scatting up a storm, Terence is leaning back in the chair, his face pointed toward the ceiling and his eyes closed, when Dad grabs his shoulder and gives him a shake. The headphones slip from his head and fall to the floor.

"Come on," Dad says. "I've been calling you."

"Sorry." Terence scoops up his headphones and follows Dad out the front door to the car, the only thing that proves for sure they used to be comfortable, happy, a family. It's Mom's car: a burgundy red, four-door sedan with heated front seats and a quality sound system. Mom was always the one who cared about music.

"What happened to your bike again?" Dad says through a yawn. He sits too close to the steering wheel, leaning over it a little, as if he still can't quite see through the haze of sleep. Of course, he's been under a haze of sleep for months now.

"'Confiscated," Terence says. "I didn't know where I was supposed to chain it up."

"Will you get it back?"

Terence shrugs. "I'm trying."

Dad nods, briefly climbing out of his haze. "Let me know if I need to call the school."

Terence thinks about the man in the front office, who always seems to be on the phone with someone. It might be the way to reach him. But no; Terence doesn't need his dad involved.

"I'll take care of it."

Dad pulls up to the curb in front of Franklin Middle and glances at the dashboard clock. "Why are you here so early?"

Terence doesn't say that he can't bear to ride the bus because only one face doesn't make him want to run and hide under his blankets. But it's the one face he truly gets sick about seeing, especially after dreaming about that face half the night.

"Gonna try to get my bike back," Terence says as he climbs out of the car. Before Dad can reply, Terence slams the door and hurries inside.

The cafeteria is serving free breakfast, and Terence can smell the pancakes and syrup and turkey sausage. The sounds of students eating echo in the empty hallways.

The office is open too and bubbling with activity, at least compared to how Terence has seen it so far. The man is there, way back from the counter, but his headset isn't on yet. Teachers of all grades and subjects — including Ms. Hardison, his first-hour teacher — mill around near the mailboxes, sipping coffee from cardboard cups and chipped novelty mugs.

Terence moves invisibly past them and right up to the counter. He leans over and says in the loudest, most confident voice he can muster, "Excuse me. How do I get my bike back?"

The man looks up. So do most of the faculty standing around him.

"Terence Kato, right?" the man says, turning his eyes to the computer display in front of him. He types a bit.

"Yes."

The man spends a minute reading the display. "Ah, here it is," the man says. "Students aren't permitted to lock up bicycles in front of the school. Ample bicycle parking is made available on the north and south walkways."

"I didn't know."

"Your student handbook states the rules very clearly, Mr. Kato," the man says, typing a bit more.

"Oh help him out, Sam," says Ms. Hardison leaning on the counter next to Terence and actually winking at him. She smells like shampoo and espresso. "He's new, and he's been through enough."

What does she know about what I've been through? Terence thinks, and then it occurs to him that she — and much of the faculty — might know quite a lot about what he's been through. They probably put stuff like that in student files.

Terence swallows and hard and scratches at a bit of dry ink on the counter.

Sam — the man at the desk — sighs and smirks and glares at Terence a minute. "You're new, so I'll give you a break — and a tip," he says. "Read your handbook. I don't want to see you in here again tomorrow because your iPod and headphones have been confiscated."

Note to self, Terence thinks. *No headphones.* Which is too bad, since the headphones now in his book bag are a major component of Operation: Avoid Talking to Eddie Because She Makes My Stomach Flip.

"I didn't know we had a handbook," Terence says.

"It was sent to your school email address when you registered," Sam says, crossing his arms and cocking his eyebrows.

"I didn't know I had a school email address," Terence says. "How do I access it?"

"Those instructions are in your handbook," Sam says.

"But how can I read the handbook if I can't," Terence starts, but the rest of his obvious question is drowned out by the first bell.

Sam rises from his seat and presents Terence with a pink form: "Confiscated item requisition form S14-A." Boxes, lines, and tiny print cover the form.

"Fill this out," Sam says, slapping a pen on the counter. "You can pick up your bike from the equipment shed on the south end of the athletic field at end of classes. Don't make me wait."

"I won't," Terence says, and he grabs the pen and glances at Ms. Hardison. "Thanks."

She winks again, grabs some papers from her mailbox, and leaves.

With the form handed in and one of his major problems hopefully solved, Terence shoulders his book bag, keeps his head down, and hurries to Ms. Hardison's class for first hour.

He zips through the front hall, keeping his eyes down, desperately trying to stay invisible.

At least it's Friday, Terence tells himself. *Then I'll have the whole weekend to figure out how to deal with the Eddie problem.*

At the bottom of the steps, though, he knocks into someone — an unfortunate side effect of keeping his head down.

"Watch it, weirdo," says a stomach-flip-inducing voice.

Terence looks up, right into Eddie's grinning face.

"You ran off pretty suddenly yesterday," she says.

"Oh, sorry," Terence says, averting his eyes and shuffling past her to the steps. "I better get going. Don't wanna be late."

"Hey!" she calls after him.

He glances back to see her standing at the

bottom of the steps, one hand on the banister, blocking traffic, but he doesn't stop.

"I *know* my singing wasn't *that* bad!" she shouts.

Terence hurries from the stairwell, slumps into his desk, and tries to catch his breath.

"Glad you made it, Terence," Ms. Hardison says from the front of the room. "Did Sam end up helping you?"

"Um, yeah," Terence says. "I'll have my bike back this afternoon."

"Good." She smiles at him and begins the day's lesson. "Now, who can tell me the difference between *rational* and *irrational*?"

Terence slumps lower in his seat. This week has gone about as irrationally as one could.

CHAPTER SIX

At lunch, sitting in the crowded cafeteria, tucked away in a corner with his hood up and his head down, Terence manages to avoid Eddie's eye.

And while he's sitting there, surrounded by all these people he doesn't know, he gets an idea: among all these other kids, surely a few must love singing.

Surely a couple must be *great* singers.

Certainly at least one must be a good singer,

who loves singing, and who won't turn up in Terence's dreams uninvited.

He takes a deep breath, leans closer to the stranger next to him — a boy in a polo shirt and khaki pants that even Terence knows are not in style — and says, "Do you know anyone in this school who likes to sing?"

"Pardon?" the boy says. He has the slightest accent, like maybe he spent a summer in England and never quite got over it.

"Someone who loves to sing?" Terence says. "Someone who might like to join a band?"

"Oh, I don't sing," the boy says. "I'm a poet."

"No, I didn't mean you," Terence says, adding quickly, "necessarily. But does anyone in school sing?"

The boy looks around over the sea of faces. "Probably," he finally says, and goes back to eating his lunch.

"Thanks," Terence says. "Very helpful."

Still, once Eddie finishes her lunch and

leaves, Terence hurries from table to table, asking if anyone knows anyone at all — in sixth, seventh, or eighth grade — who sings. He gets a few names, and meets a few people, and when the bell rings to end the hour, he feels a bit better, like maybe he won't be stuck in a band with Eddie.

In fact, he's almost smiling as he leaves the cafeteria, but the moment he steps into the hall, Eddie stops him with a stiff palm to his chest.

"Weirdo," she says, as if it's his name.

"Oh," Terence says. "Hi."

"Are you avoiding me?" she asks.

Terence shakes his head and spits.

"Are you?" she says again.

"How do you do that?" Terence finally says. "How do you just come out and say what you're thinking?"

"What else would I say?"

"I don't know," Terence admits. "Nothing. I'd say nothing."

"You're good at that," Eddie says, laughing a little.

"I have to get to my next class," Terence says, dropping his head and starting off.

But Eddie grabs his book bag and stops him. "Hold up," she says. "You've been asking literally everyone in school if they know any singers."

"How do you know that?" Terence asks.

She shrugs. "I guess people know I like to sing," she says, "so a few people mentioned it."

"Word travels fast."

"So?" she says, pointing her chin at him. "You don't want me in the band."

"It's not like that," Terence says, starting to walk off again.

Eddie hurries alongside. "Then what?" she says. "You need backup singers too?"

"No."

"Then what?"

Terence stops and glares at her. He retreats

into a corner. "Look, I like the way you sing, OK?" he says quietly. "A lot."

"Thanks."

Terence looks at his sneakers. "And I like *you*," he says, quieter still, so she has to lean down a little to hear him, "a lot."

"So what's the problem?" Eddie says. "So we play music and have fun. We've got a band. Or a duo of friends, anyway. It's a good start."

"I don't *want* friends, Eddie," he says, finally looking into her eyes.

"Why not?" she asks, not understanding.

The truth is, Terence doesn't fully understand either, and when Eddie puts the question to him like that, he's forced to think about why for the first time.

"Because this school," he says slowly, his mind far away, "my time here, the band I want to put together . . . none of it's real."

"Um," she says, "I feel pretty real." She grabs her cheek and gives it a pinch. "Yup. Real."

"For you," Terence says. "But for me?" He thinks about his mom and her sickness and the months since, and it's all he can do not to cry in front of her, so he just shakes his head again.

Eddie's face falls. For the first time since he met her, it's not grinning or scowling or snarling. It's just sad.

"Sorry," he says.

Now Eddie is the one who can't speak. She shakes her head. "Let me join the band."

"Of course," he says. "Obviously you're in the band. I'm sorry for — for avoiding you, for hiding."

"I get it," she says. "You don't have to explain."

"Thanks."

Around them, the halls have emptied. Only a few voices and stray footsteps remain. "Now we really better get to class," Eddie says. "Mr. Amal is gonna kill me if I'm late for bio again."

She backs away, her eyes still on Terence.

"You OK?" she asks.

Terence nods and forces a smile.

"Good," she says as she skips away toward the science wing. "And don't worry about us being friends," she adds over her shoulder, that playful grin returning to her face. "I don't like you that much anyway."

Terence can't help laughing as Eddie disappears around the corner. He wipes at his eyes to make sure they're tear-free, and then turns the corner toward Language Arts class — and right into the broad chest and gritted teeth of one saxophone-playing brother named Luke.

"Sorry," Terence says.

Luke gives him a light shove — light but hard enough to knock Terence stumbling backward. "If you hurt my sister," Luke says, "I'll hurt you back."

"Hurt her?" Terence says, backing away a little more. "She's bigger than me!"

Luke snarls.

"Look, we're just going to play music together," Terence says, hands up and still backing away. "Nothing else going on here."

Luke growls and closes the gap between them.

"Really," Terence insists. "You have nothing to worry about."

Luke bears his teeth.

"And I'm going to be late for Language Arts!" Terence says. With that, he dodges to the right, runs past Luke, and takes off down the hall and into his classroom.

Terence drops into his desk at the back of the class and mutters to himself, "Life here is going to be interesting."

MUSIC TRIVIA

Think you have what it takes to join Terence Kato's band? Take this music trivia quiz and find out!

1. What is the level and intensity of sound measured in?
   A. Decibels
   B. Gigabytes
   C. Vibrato

2. A musical scale comprises how many notes?
   A. 16
   B. 8
   C. 10

3. What term describes people singing without instruments?
   A. Solo
   B. Allegro
   C. A cappella

4. What term describes the section of a song that is repeated after each verse?
   A. Beat
   B. Chorus
   C. Choir

5. What term describes how high or low a musical sound is?
   A. Pitch
   B. Range
   C. Volume

6. What is the highest singing voice called?
   A. Baritone
   B. Tenor
   C. Soprano

7. How many musical instruments make up a quartet?
   A. 4
   B. 14
   C. 8

8. What Italian word means "growing louder?"
   A. Crescendo
   B. Bass
   C. Allegro

9. What are all instruments that are played by being hit with something called?
   A. Brass
   B. Woodwinds
   C. Percussion

10. What is the lowest singing voice called?
    A. Baritone
    B. Tenor
    C. Soprano

Answers: 1. A 2. B 3. C 4. B 5. A 6. C
7. A 8. A 9. C 10. A

Read the entire series

BOY SEEKING BAND

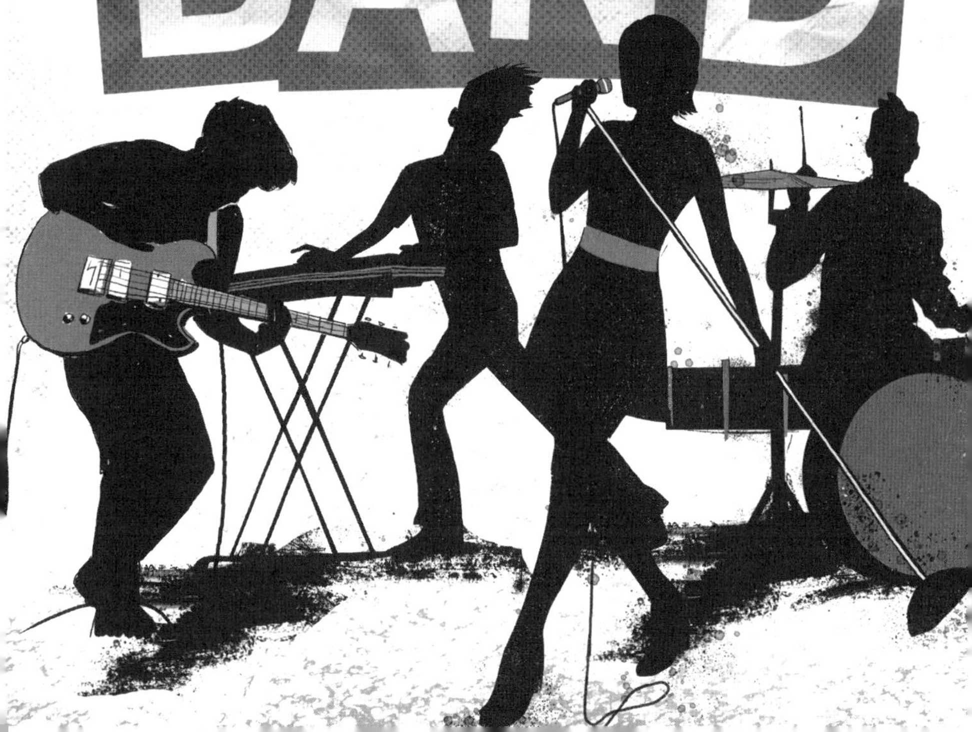

STEVE BREZENOFF

Steve Brezenoff is the author of more than fifty middle-grade chapter books, including the Field Trip Mysteries series, the Ravens Pass series of thrillers, and the Return to the Titanic series. He's also written three young-adult novels, *Guy in Real Life*; *Brooklyn, Burning*; and *The Absolute Value of -1*. In his spare time, he enjoys video games, cycling, and cooking. Steve lives in Minneapolis with his wife, Beth, and their son and daughter.